BUNNY MONEY

By Stephen Krensky

Illustrated by Emily Bolam

LITTLE SIMON
An imprint of Simon & Schuster Children's Publishing Division
New York   London   Toronto   Sydney
1230 Avenue of the Americas, New York, New York 10020
Text copyright © 2011 by Stephen Krensky. Illustrations copyright © 2011 by Emily Bolam
All rights reserved, including the right of reproduction in whole or in part in any form.
LITTLE SIMON is a registered trademark of Simon & Schuster, Inc., and associated colophon is a
trademark of Simon & Schuster, Inc. For information about special discounts for bulk purchases,
please contact Simon & Schuster Special Sales at 1-866-506-1949 or business@simonandschuster.com.
The Simon & Schuster Speakers Bureau can bring authors to your live event.
For more information or to book an event contact the Simon & Schuster Speakers Bureau
at 1-866-248-3049 or visit our website at www.simonspeakers.com.
Manufactured in China 1110 LEO
First Edition
2 4 6 8 10 9 7 5 3 1
ISBN 978-1-4424-0888-3

Acorn, Basil, Clover, and Daisy were shopping for their mother's birthday present.

"Look!" cried Acorn, pointing to a store window.

"That's a beautiful hat," said Basil.

"Mama would like it," said Clover.

"But it costs one dollar," said Daisy. "Do we have that much?"

Nobody was sure.

The bunnies went inside the store.

"We want to buy the hat in the window," Acorn told the clerk.
"But we don't know if we have enough money," said Basil.
"Well," said the clerk, "let's find out."

Acorn emptied her pockets on the counter.
She had a flower and a bunch of pennies.
"A flower isn't money," said Basil,
as the clerk counted the pennies.

"But it's pretty," said Clover.
"And twenty-five pennies
is a good start," said the clerk.

= 25¢

Basil emptied his pockets too.
He had two buttons and five
nickels.
"I wondered where I put those
buttons," he said.

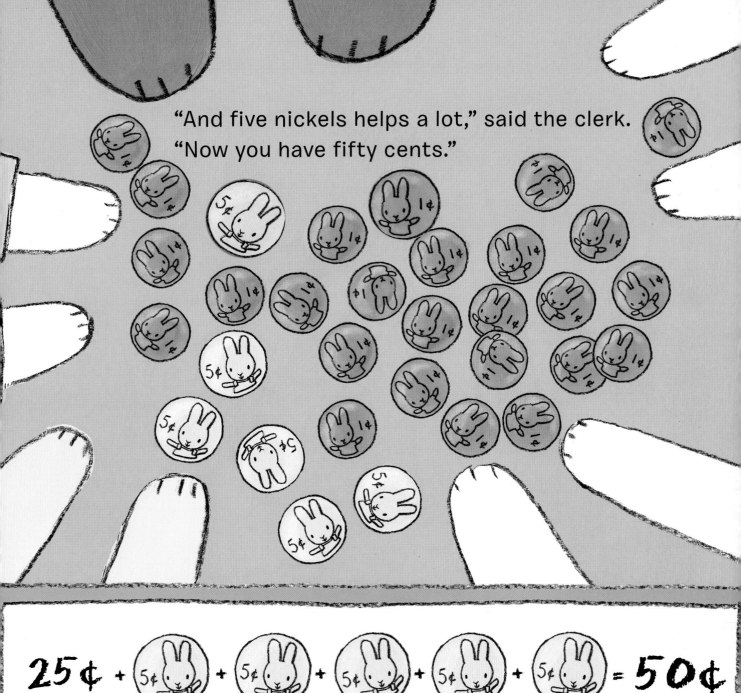

"And five nickels helps a lot," said the clerk.
"Now you have fifty cents."

25¢ + 5¢ + 5¢ + 5¢ + 5¢ + 5¢ = 50¢

Then Clover took out a carrot, two dimes, and a nickel.
She brushed off the carrot. "I don't suppose we could
sell this," she said.

"No," said the clerk, "but with two dimes and a nickel you now have seventy-five cents."

50¢ +

+ 10¢ + 10¢

+ 5¢

= 75¢

"I'm next," said Daisy. She took out an old brass key.
"I wish this could unlock a treasure chest," she said.
"Me too," said Acorn.
"Is there anything else?" asked Basil.
"Just this one quarter," Daisy said. "That's all."

The clerk smiled. "With that last quarter, you have one hundred cents. That's exactly one dollar."

"Hooray!" cried the bunnies.

75¢
+
25¢
=
$1

So Acorn, Basil, Clover, and Daisy brought the hat home.

"*Happy birthday, Mama!*" they shouted.

"What's this?" asked their mama.

"We bought it with our bunny money," said Clover.

"It added up perfectly," said Daisy.

"You know what?" said their mama. "I think my four bunnies add up perfectly, too." And she gave them all a great big hug.